Magic in the Garden

Magic in the Garden

by

Cynthia L. Hart

Magic is always around us —
May you always enjoy life —

Cynthia Hart

DORRANCE PUBLISHING CO., INC.
PITTSBURGH, PENNSYLVANIA 15222

ISBN # 0-8059-5037-0
Printed in the United States of America

First Printing

For information or to order additional books, please write:
Dorrance Publishing Co., Inc.
643 Smithfield Street
Pittsburgh, Pennsylvania 15222
U.S.A.
1-800-788-7654

To my grandchildren, Cynthia, Deven, Samuel, and Vai, for the magic you bring into my life. To Leo, whose encouragement and love made all things possible.

In a large yellow house in the country lived a small boy with his mother, father, and little brother. The little boy's name was Deven, and he was three years old. Deven was a happy boy with many toys, but his favorite thing to do was to explore the garden in the backyard. There were flowers and bugs and, on occasion, at just the right time of day, something magic happens.

It was the first day of spring when Deven noticed that his garden was different from everybody else's. It was just

before dinner, and he was playing on his slide. Mother told him that he would have to come in for dinner in about twenty minutes. Deven wished his brother were bigger so that he could play outside on the slide, too.

He heard the breeze blow through the trees and move over the flowers in the garden. All of a sudden Deven noticed a beautiful butterfly in the flowers. He hurried down the slide and ran to the flower bed. The butterfly didn't move. That was unusual because butterflies usually flew away when Deven came near them.

As Deven got closer he noticed that this butterfly was different from all the others he had seen. This one had arms and legs just like his, and it had on a pink dress and had long golden hair. The butterfly's wings were all the colors of the rainbow and you could see right through them. Deven said, "What a beautiful butterfly!"

To Deven's surprise, the butterfly laughed and said, "Oh, no, Deven! I'm

Gwendolyn the Garden Fairy. I'm one of the 'Wee People' who take care of the garden." Now Deven was really confused. Why hadn't Mother told him that there were "Wee People" in the garden?

Deven asked Gwendolyn, "May I meet the other Wee People? Would they play with me, and could I help them in the garden?"

The fairy replied, "You must be very quiet if you want to meet the others." Gwendolyn told Deven that the Wee People could use his help because he was so much bigger than any of them.

Gwendolyn waved her magic wand and told the other Wee People to come out. Deven watched as small faces appeared in the roses, daffodils, daisies, and other garden flowers. Under the moss-covered rock wall Deven saw two small men. They were bigger than the fairies. Gwendolyn introduced George and Gordon Gnome to Deven. They were very cute and wore green shirts, red

pants, and shoes that had pointed toes. Deven was surprised that they were just as tall as his knees.

Suddenly Deven saw a golden light flash across the fish pond. Gwendolyn said, "This is Walter the Water Sprite. It is Walter's job to make certain that the garden has enough water." The water sprite moved very quickly from flower to flower. As his wings moved, droplets of water fell on the flowers' upturned faces. As each flower was visited, the flower would smile and say, "Thank you, Walter." Deven didn't know that flowers could smile.

Just then Deven's mother called him to come in for dinner. Where had all the time gone? He turned to his new friends and asked, "Will you be here to play with me tomorrow?"

Gwendolyn replied, "Don't worry, we will be waiting for you after your nap." With that Deven said goodbye and went into dinner. All through dinner he wondered if

he should tell his parents about his new friends. He decided it would be his secret, and he wouldn't even tell his brother Vai.

That evening after Deven had his bath, and his mother was reading him a story before bedtime, he asked, "Mother, do you believe in fairies and the Wee People?"

Deven's mother smiled and said, "Where did you hear about fairies and the Wee People?"

He didn't answer her. Instead he said, "Mother, do you believe?"

"Yes, Deven, I believe," said Mother. He kissed his mother, snuggled down under his covers, and went to sleep. Mother kissed him again, smiling, and thought, *Fairies and the Wee People, indeed.*

Several hours later Deven was awakened by a tapping at his window. He sat up in his bed and looked around. To his amazement, George and Gordon Gnome

were at his window waving at him to come to the garden. Deven got out of bed and went to the window. It was dark outside, but the garden sparkled with many tiny lights as fairies scurried around the garden tending to each flower. George and Gordon seemed to need his help right now!

Quietly Deven went downstairs, crossed the family room, and went out the patio door. George and Gordon were waiting for him. "What's the matter?" Deven asked.

George and Gordon looked at each other and exclaimed, "The gopher has made a big hole next to our Rose, and we are afraid that the gopher will eat her!

"We need your help to move a rock over the large hole to make the gopher go away." All the fairies and the water sprite flew close to Deven, hovering there to see if he would help save Rose.

"I'm so small—do you think I can help?" he asked.

George and Gordon took his hands and said, "Please, friend, we need you, or we will lose our Rose."

Deven moved toward the garden, even though he knew he would be in trouble if he got dirty on top of being awake when he should have been asleep and outside when he should have been in bed. The three friends hurried to Rose. Deven could see the large hole made by the gopher. He knew where they could find a rock just the right size. As he bent over to take a closer look at the hole, he noticed a wonderful fragrance. He looked at Rose and she smiled at him with a smile like he had only seen from his mother—that smile that says, "I know you can do it, because I love you." Deven touched Rose gently with his finger and said, "Don't worry, we'll protect you."

With Deven leading the way, the three friends found the rock. Now, how to get it to the hole? All the fairies and the water sprite were giving Deven ideas.

Then he saw his little red wagon. With help from everyone they managed to get the rock into the wagon. George, Gordon, and Deven pulled and pulled until they had the wagon very close to the rose bed. They lifted and lifted the rock until they had the rock out of the wagon. Then they rolled and rolled the rock until the hole was covered.

Everyone cheered, "Rose is safe! Deven is our hero!" All the Wee People made a circle around Deven, and Gwendolyn flew over them dropping sparkling fairy dust. It was a wonderful celebration but Deven was very sleepy. He said goodnight and very quietly went back in the house, up the stairs, and into his room. As he crawled into his bed he didn't notice how dirty he had gotten his pajamas. All he could see were the fairies at his window saying goodnight.

In the morning Deven's mother came to his room to wake him. She kissed him softly as he stirred and then he smiled up at his mother.

"Deven, how did you get your pajamas so dirty?" she asked.

As he was thinking about how he was going to answer his mother and explain his great adventure, he noticed that someone had put a single yellow rose on his night stand. He reached over, took the rose in his small hand, and with great pride said, "Why, Mother, I was helping save this for you."

Deven's mother started to ask him another question, but instead she took the rose, gave him a kiss, and wondered what he had been up to. *Still,* she thought, *how sweet—a rose from my little man.*

As the day went on Deven kept asking if he could play in the garden. Mother told him he would have to wait until after his nap. So Deven helped his mother and played with his brother Vai.

When Deven awoke from his nap he hurried to put on his shoes and went outside. Mother watched from the door as he ran to the moss-covered rock wall calling George and Gordon. When no one came, Mother closed the door and went to do the laundry. She would check on Deven in a little while.

Deven looked all over the garden but didn't see his friends anywhere. He checked Rose to be sure the rock was still in place. There was the rock, but where were his friends? Deven became sad and started to cry. Just then he heard a soft whisper. "Deven! Psst! Deven!" As he wiped his tears and looked up he found that the fairies had encircled him. The water sprite flew by and droplets of water fell on his head. He clapped his hands with joy. Deven listened carefully and could hear the other fairies in the garden. But where were George and Gordon?

He decided to play on his slide. As he reached the top of the ladder he found

George and Gordon waiting for him. Deven laughed and laughed as they hooked themselves together like a train and down the slide they went over and over again.

Mother and Vai heard the laughter and came to the door to see what Deven was doing. Imagine their surprise—there was Deven with George and Gordon Gnome while all around them the fairies and the water sprite were flying in the air. Deven was surrounded by beautiful colors and twinkling lights—a gift from the fairies for helping them save Rose.

The three friends saw Mother and Vai smiling and laughing. They waved at Mother, and she waved back. Mother felt a soft breeze and droplets of water on her face. She looked up and saw Walter the Water Sprite. Gwendolyn the Garden Fairy and Walter the Water Sprite thanked Mother for Deven's help in the garden. Now Mother knew how his pajamas got so dirty. Mother and Vai joined

him and his friends in the garden and watched as he played with his new friends.

As twilight came, Deven, Vai, and Mother had to leave the garden to go inside. "Tomorrow is another day, Deven, and you will see your friends again," Mother said.

Deven asked, "Mother, where do the Wee People come from?"

Mother looked down at his tiny face and said, "They come from the goodness of your heart."

That evening after Deven and Vai had fallen asleep Mother went to the window and looked down at the garden. She thought about this magical place. As she stood there quietly watching she saw little fairy lights moving about. Mother felt a water droplet on her cheek, but this time it wasn't from Walter the Water Sprite—it was a tear of joy and happiness.

Mother looked at the garden one last time. George and Gordon Gnome waved

at her and blew her a kiss. Mother waved back. *It's Deven's magic in the garden,* she thought. *I do believe and always will!*